100% UNOFFICIAL

MRBEAST

First published in Great Britain 2024 by
DEAN, part of Farshore
An imprint of HarperCollins*Publishers*
1 London Bridge Street, London SE1 9GF
www.farshore.co.uk

HarperCollins*Publishers*
Macken House, 39/40 Mayor Street Upper, Dublin 1, D01 C9W8, Ireland

Written by Ben Wilson

This book is an original creation by Farshore © 2024 HarperCollins*Publishers* Limited

ISBN: 978 0 00 871477 2
Printed in Italy
001

All rights reserved. No part of this publication may be reproduced, stored in a retrieval system, or transmitted in any form or by any means, electronic, mechanical, photocopying, recording or otherwise, without the prior permission of the publisher and copyright owner.

This book is 100% independent and unofficial and is not endorsed by and has no connection with the people or persons featured, or with any organization or individual connected in any way whatsoever with the people or persons featured. Every care has been taken in the researching and writing of this book but due to the nature of the subject matter some information may change over time.

ONLINE SAFETY FOR YOUNGER FANS

Spending time online is great fun! Here are a few simple rules to help younger fans stay safe and keep the internet a great place to spend time:

- Never give out your real name – don't use it as your username.
- Never give out any of your personal details.
- Never tell anybody which school you go to or how old you are.
- Never tell anybody your password except a parent or a guardian.
- Be aware that you must be 13 or over to create an account on many sites. Always check the site policy and ask a parent or guardian for permission before registering.
- Always tell a parent or guardian if something is worrying you. Stay safe online. Any website addresses listed in this book are correct at the time of going to print. However, Farshore is not responsible for content hosted by third parties. Please be aware that online content can be subject to change and websites can contain content that is unsuitable for children. We advise that all children are supervised when using the internet.

Stay safe online. Farshore is not responsible for content hosted by third parties.

This book contains FSC™ certified paper and other controlled sources to ensure responsible forest management.

For more information visit: www.harpercollins.co.uk/green

100% UNOFFICIAL

MRBEAST

THE UNOFFICIAL GUIDE TO YOUTUBE'S BIGGEST STAR

Contents

This Is MrBeast	6
MrBeast Channel Guide	8
MrBeast Around The World	10
All About The Beast Gang	12
Top Five Most Watched	14
MrBeast Timeline	16
All About MrBeast Philanthropy	18
Top Five Coolest Collabs	20
MrBeast's Biggest Awards	22
All About Feastables	24
Top Five Travel Tales	26
MrBeast, Record Breaker	28
All About Video Games	30
Top Five Crazy Challenges	32
MrBeast In Numbers	34
All About MrBeast's Hometown	36

Top Five Spooky Scares	38
MrBeast's Movie Moments	40
All About Beast Gang Gross-Outs	42
Top Five Greatest Giveaways	44
At Home With MrBeast	46
All About Team Trees & Team Seas	48
Top Five Toy Stories	50
MrBeast's Abandoned City	52
All About Sports	54
Top Five Guests & Rivals	56
Happy Birthday, MrBeast!	58
All About Celebrity Friends	60
Top Five Animal Moments	62
MrBeast's Best Quotes	64
All About MrBeast's Projects	66
Top Five Food Frenzies	68
MrBeast's Essential Trivia	70
Credits	72

This Is MrBeast

The key facts you need to know about the coolest guy on YouTube!

Book: The 7 Habits of Highly Effective People by Stephen Covey. MrBeast loves reading advice about what makes us successful, and then applying it to himself.

Real Name: James "Jimmy" Stephen Donaldson
Height: 6'2"
Birthday: 7 May 1998
Born: Wichita, Kansas, USA

Gamer Tag: It was originally MrBeast6000. He got rid of the 6000 and the name we all know him by was born!

Favorite Color: Blue. He revealed it in a *Minecraft* short. That explains why it's the main color in the MrBeast logo!

Drink: Cirkul water. It comes in a special bottle that lets you add a flavor before each sip.

100% UNOFFICIAL

Food: Sushi, Feastables chocolate (obvs), and his mom's teriyaki chicken!

Role Model: Apple creator Steve Jobs, for his unrelenting passion towards making the best product ever.

Video Games: Call of Duty, Minecraft, Among Us, and Fortnite. His all-time fave is League of Legends!

Animal: His dog Pinky, who is a mix of breeds. He adopted her with his girlfriend as part of the 'I Adopted Every Dog In A Dog Shelter' video, where he helped fourteen dogs find new homes!

Fave YouTube Channels: PolyMatter, Wendover Productions, Mark Rober, and Veritasium. He says he just loves to learn new things!

Film: Toy Story, because it was made during Steve Jobs' Pixar days!

Charity: MrBeast is famed for his philanthropic projects, such as Team Trees and Team Seas. He's raised more than $56 million for those alone!

MrBeast Channel Guide

MrBeast has five main active channels. Here's what happens on each one, from wild challenges to generous giveaways!

In 'Protect $500,000 to Keep It,' MrBeast's friend Blake planned to build a fortress of vehicles.

MrBeast

MrBeast's main hub is the most subscribed YouTube channel in the world! It had 285 million subscribers by June 2024, after finally beating rival T-Series to the top spot. It's the main home for all his stunts, giveaways, and challenges. But when it launched in 2012, it was mainly focused on video games like *Minecraft*!

Beast Reacts

MrBeast launched his second channel, originally named BeastHacks, in 2016. After a year away, it relaunched in 2021. Since then, the channel features videos of MrBeast and Kris reacting to trick shots and experiments. Ever wondered what would happen if one tank went up against ten cars? Beast Reacts has the answer!

Karl joins Beast Reacts to compete in reactions to WhistlinDiesel's '7 Trucks vs Monstermax' video.

100% UNOFFICIAL

The Beast Gang loves an explosion! Karl is setting off masses of Minecraft TNT in MrBeast Gaming.

Old and Secret Channels

How many have you heard of?!

MrBeast 3
MrBeast Extra
Beast
Totally Not MrBeast
Beast Network
MrBeast5997
MrBeast5998
MeTalkOverGames
CurrentContent

MrBeast 2

MrBeast 2 is actually his fourth YouTube Channel and features all the funny vids he can't squeeze in elsewhere. It's mostly TikTok-style shorts of the crew pulling hilarious antics, like getting the world's highest-paid hand model to hold melted Feastables chocolate! If you're looking for quick laughs in a phone-friendly format, this is the channel for you.

MrBeast Gaming

Karl, Kris, and Chandler all star alongside MrBeast on his dedicated gaming channel. It launched in 2020 with lots of content devoted to *Minecraft*. Other favorites include *Among Us* and *Roblox*. Its most popular video is creating the 'World's Largest Explosion' in *Minecraft*. It's been watched 199 million times!

MrBeast hired the world's highest paid hand model to star in this gooey Feastables video on MrBeast 2.

Beast Philanthropy

This isn't just a channel but a charity, too. MrBeast is known as one of the world's most generous celebrities. His videos for good causes go here. Memorable moments include giving 20,000 pairs of shoes to children in South Africa, feeding 10,000 families for Thanksgiving, and donating $3 million worth of aid to Ukrainian refugees.

MrBeast Around The World

MrBeast's rapid rise has taken him around the globe and back again. Which places do you recognize from his videos?!

Mansfield, Ohio, USA

The super spooky Ohio State Reformatory, where MrBeast filmed 'We Spent 24 Hours In The Most Haunted Place On Earth', is here. It closed in 1990 and is now famous for movies like *The Shawshank Redemption*!

Wichita, Kansas, USA

James "Jimmy" Stephen Donaldson, AKA MrBeast, was born here on 7 May 1998. It's a city with a population of 397,000 people. Many call it the 'Air Capital' of the world, because so many planes have been built there!

CocoCay, Bahamas

The ending of '$1 vs $250,000,000 Private Island' was filmed here! It really did cost that much to build and mainly hosts passengers stopping off on super-expensive Caribbean cruises.

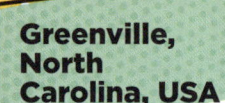

Greenville, North Carolina, USA

This is where MrBeast grew up and is now home to his HQ. Not only that, videos such as 'I Built Willy Wonka's Chocolate Factory' were filmed here, too.

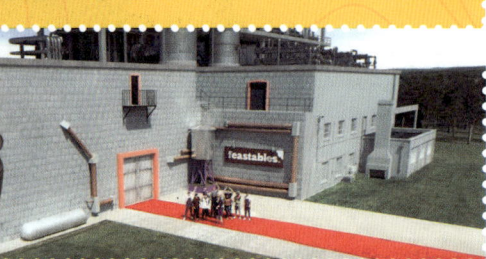

100% UNOFFICIAL

Southend, England

MrBeast has been to the UK! Essex received a visit from the legend when he filmed 'Last To Take Hand Off Jet, Keeps It'. Twelve YouTubers battled to win their own plane!

Paris, France

Beast Gang headed here for part of the '$1 vs $250,000 Vacation' video. They got to climb all the way up the Eiffel Tower, then turned off all the lights once at the top!

Kupari, Croatia

This is the location where MrBeast filmed 'I Survived 7 Days In An Abandoned City'. Despite most of its buildings being empty, around 950 people still live here!

Bucharest, Romania

In one of his biggest acts of generosity, MrBeast donated $3 million worth of aid to Ukrainian refugees. His rep Darren flew to Romania to help distribute food, medical supplies, and other essential items.

Tripoli, Libya

Home city of Alla Nasser, who beat Slovenia to win the 'Every Country On Earth Fights For $250,000' challenge. These days he lives in New York!

Tokyo, Japan

The Beast Gang's most expensive stop on their '$1 vs $250,000 Vacation' journey. They stayed in the country's poshest hotel and drove real Mario karts through the streets of Tokyo!

ALL ABOUT
The Beast Gang

Everything you need to know about MrBeast's cool—and always hilarious—crew!

When Kris took a lie detector test for a video, she answered questions like, "Was Jimmy a good roommate?"

Kris

Name Kris Tyson
Birthday 1 July 1996
Height 5'11"
Hair Brown **Eyes** Blue

Kris is a school friend of MrBeast and was his first ever subscriber! The pair have been pulling pranks on one another since those early days. She's the main host of the Beast Reacts channel and her Insta account has more than 2.4 million followers! In 2023, Kris came out publicly as a transgender woman in an interview with Anthony Padilla, saying, "I'm still the same person, I just look a little different."

One of the first, and biggest, challenges that Chandler won was 'Last To Leave $800,000 Island Keeps It.'

Chandler

Name Chandler Hallow **Birthday** 3 December 1998
Height 6'4" **Hair** Smoky blonde **Eyes** Brown

Before he got famous, Chandler was actually the on-set cleaner for MrBeast's videos! Fans enjoy his funny fears, like gherkins—he wouldn't even eat one for $5,000! He also has a rare type of color blindness called Achromatopsia. This means he can only see black, white and grey. Chandler's also insanely good at challenges, he's won more than $3 million in games such as 'Last To Leave $800,000 Island Keeps It'!

THE BIG GANG
The Beast Gang aren't the only ones helping to create MrBeast videos. There are currently over 250 people working on his channels and content.

12

100% UNOFFICIAL

Nolan

Name Nolan Hansen **Birthday** 1 June 1998
Height 6'1" **Hair** Light brown **Eyes** Blue

Nolan ran a YouTube channel called TrendCave before becoming the fifth member of MrBeast's crew. He's found victories hard to come by but did triumph in the 'First To Rob Bank Wins $100,000' challenge! The crew loves to make fun of him and he usually takes it well. Although, technically, he should be in solitary confinement until 2041 as punishment for his prison escape attempt in another video!

Nolan was the winner of the challenge to rob a bank vault and went home with $100,000!

Karl always jumps into new challenges, even if it means getting his hands (and clothes) messy!

Karl

Name Karl Jacobs
Birthday 19 July 1998
Height 5'11"
Hair Brown **Eyes** Grey

Karl first popped up on 'Last To Leave Halloween Candy Wins $10,000', a challenge by MrBro (MrBeast's brother). Before that, he had a YouTube channel called Game Patrol, focused on Roblox! He's now legendary for his Minecraft content. Karl replaced original MrBeast crew member Jake The Viking in 2020. He took the job with MrBeast just five weeks before he was due to finish college!

Tareq

Name Tareq Salameh
Birthday 9 December 1994
Height Unknown
Hair Black **Eyes** Brown

Tareq is MrBeast's head cameraman. Many fans consider him the unsung hero of the gang! He was born in Saudi Arabia and grew up in the USA. Tareq made a fortune from one of MrBeast's cleverest clips. 'If You Click This Video I'll Give My Friend $0.001' scored 200 million views, earning Tareq a very tasty $200,000!

Even now, every time this video gets a view, MrBeast gives Tareq $0.001. It adds up!

TOP FIVE

Most Watched

HITTING HIGH
The combined views of these videos (counted in June 2024) is 2.16 billion and they're climbing every day. Imagine what they'll be in a year!

Incredibly, some MrBeast videos have screamed past 300 million views! These are the five seen more than any others...

Contestants were given personalized clothes and given the option to play games to win.

1
$1 vs $1,000,000 Hotel Room
Views: 349 million

MrBeast's hotel mission is all about showing off the comfort that money can buy. He started off by renting a mat in India for $1 a night and then worked his way up through pricier options. For $1,000, the gang stayed 200 feet below ground, in a cave. Meanwhile, for $10,000, they chilled out underwater, with fish swimming overhead.

2
Ages 1 - 100 Fight For $500,000
Views: 375 million

Could you be the last person standing for half a million dollars? MrBeast put one person for each age, from one to 100, into glass cubes. The 100-year-old got a giant applause when he left. Ages 52 and 40 were the final two, after more than a week. It came down to choosing one of two golden suitcases and Joe, AKA number 40, won!

Nolan, Chandler, and MrBeast searched for interesting fish in their underwater hotel.

100% UNOFFICIAL

3 $1 vs $500,000 Plane Ticket
Views: 384 million

Everyone loves a holiday, so MrBeast tried the cheapest plane in the world, a $10,000 first-class trip, and a journey on a private jet! Obviously, the last one was the most interesting. The gang had to remove their shoes after boarding to protect the swanky carpets! It had its own mini cinema, a lounge for twelve people, and even gold-plated sinks in the bathrooms.

Kris and Nolan checked out the twelve-person lounge while the rest of the team took a tour.

4 Last To Leave Circle Wins $500,000
Views: 442 million

Early in the challenge, the contestants had a giant circle to stand in but it was slowly cut down.

One big red circle, 100 people, and a massive pile of money for the last person standing. Some competitors lasted over a week, despite the circle shrinking daily and temptations along the way. The first person to leave got a new car! Survival was hard, especially when Karl played a phone alarm for ten hours straight. There was even a marriage proposal!

5 $456,000 Squid Game In Real Life
Views: 616 million

This is MrBeast's most popular video ever! It recreated a grown-up survival show. 456 people battled for the big prize, in games like Honeycomb, where players had to make a specific shape out of a cookie, without it breaking up! Sets looked just like the real TV show. It all came down to a game of musical chairs, which contestant 79 won!

Karl and Kris selected the music for the final round of musical chairs in MrBeast's Squid Game.

MrBeast Timeline

How MrBeast gradually took over YouTube, year by year!

2017

MrBeast goes viral thanks to his 'I Counted To 100,000' video. He builds on that by recording loads of stunts and challenges, like 'Spinning A Fidget Spinner For 24 Hours Straight'. He doesn't manage the full day but over eleven hours is still incredible! He banks 1 million subscribers.

1998

James "Jimmy" Donaldson is born in Wichita, Kansas on 7 May. His family moves around a lot and eventually settles in Greenville, North Carolina. He grows up close to his older brother, CJ, who also later achieves YouTube fame as MrBro / CJTheseDays!

2016

MrBeast's popularity starts to increase thanks to his 'Worst Intros On YouTube' series. He drops out of East Carolina University to focus on YouTube full time and passes 30,000 subscribers.

2012

At the age of 13, MrBeast starts posting YouTube videos. They're focused on games like *Minecraft* and guessing what influencers earn. He soon shortens his original name of MrBeast6000, to make it catchier!

100% UNOFFICIAL

2019

Former space engineer Mark Rober teams up with MrBeast to create Team Trees. Their aim is to raise $20 million by the end of the year for the Arbor Day Foundation, which is dedicated to planting new trees. They hit the target in just two months!

2020

MrBeast has his first go at entering the food market with MrBeast Burger. He also wins Creator of the Year at the Streamy Awards. What he doesn't know is that he'll also win it in 2021, 2022, and 2023!

2021

'$456,000 Squid Game In Real Life' is uploaded to YouTube and takes MrBeast to yet another level. In one week, it receives over 130 million views. It goes on to be his most popular video ever, with a total of 616 million views over the next three years!

2024

Another huge landmark gets smashed as MrBeast becomes the most subscribed YouTube channel in the world in June 2024. His main channel overtakes T-Series, an Indian music label, which had held the most-subscribed record for five years!

2022

It's food fun time again, as MrBeast launches his own chocolate brand: Feastables! American experts Forbes rank him as the highest earning YouTuber, after making $54 million in one year. Second is Jake Paul ($45 million), while Markiplier is third ($38 million). He also soars past 100 million subscribers.

ALL ABOUT MrBeast Philanthropy

MrBeast is one of the most generous celebrities on the planet. These are just a few of his kindest moments ...

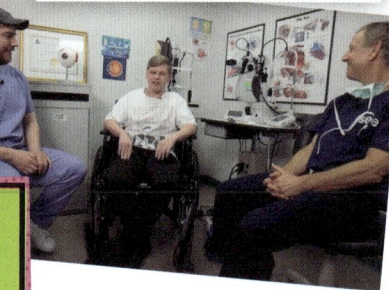

While helping fund 100 surgeries, MrBeast met with some of the patients and doctors.

As part of his aim to help provide clean drinking water, MrBeast filmed this video to build more awarenesss about the organizations.

Helping the Blind

Astonishingly, MrBeast helped 100 blind people see again. He paid for operations where a surgeon removes someone's damaged eye lens, then replaces it with an artificial one. It only takes ten minutes but is far too expensive for most people. As well as helping those in the United States, he provided surgery in countries like Namibia, Jamaica, and Honduras too.

Building African Wells

MrBeast helped 500,000 people across Cameroon, Kenya, Somalia, Uganda, and Zimbabwe. He launched a fundraiser for local water aid organizations and built 100 wells, helping provide clean drinking water. That wasn't all. MrBeast also delivered bikes to a village in Zimbabwe to help children get to school and donated furniture and computers to Kenyan schools.

Rebuilding Homes

A bird's eye view of the devastated city that MrBeast and his team helped to rebuild.

In December 2021, a hurricane tore through Kentucky in the USA. MrBeast jumped into action, sending his team to help rebuild houses and push the local government to provide skilled builders, so the process would go faster. Once they were fixed up, he also made sure that every home was equipped with new furniture!

100% UNOFFICIAL

Acting Like Father Christmas

MrBeast didn't attempt to grow Santa Claus's white beard. But everything else about his impersonation was spot-on, as he gave 10,000 presents to kids in need. The Beast Gang visited New York, Tennessee, New Mexico, and California to drop off gifts to children's hospitals. Then they took blankets, socks, and gloves to homeless shelters, to make sure adults in need also had a happy Christmas.

MrBeast tried out Father Christmas's style, both the outfit and gift-giving!

Aiding Amputees

MrBeast teamed up with a charity called Exceed Worldwide to help Cambodian amputees walk again. The country has major problems with land mines from a war in the 1960s, which still explode occasionally. MrBeast paid for 2,000 prosthetic limbs. He also donated over $200 to keep the island's two clinics open for at least a year.

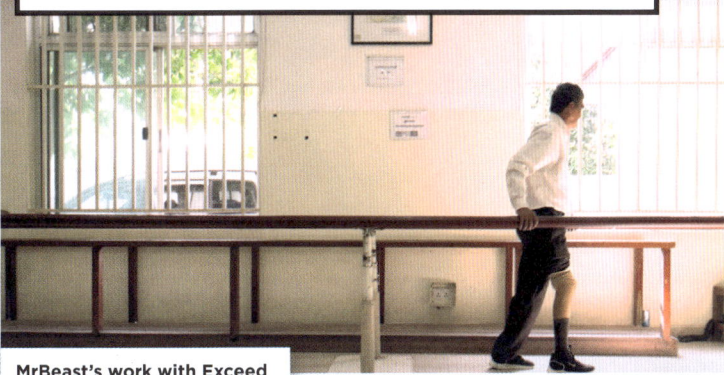

MrBeast's work with Exceed Worldwide has given 2,000 people new prosthetic limbs.

Stopping Food Waste

Sharing Excess is a charity that stops food from going to waste. It works with restaurants and grocery stores to find homes for unused ingredients and meals. MrBeast partnered with them and managed to save over 4.5 million kgs of food in a year! Instead of being wasted, it went to shelters and families in need.

Restaurants and grocery stores donate their excess food to charity to cut down on waste.

Plus this stuff, too ...

Donating Toys
A hospital of poorly children were given a touch of hope when MrBeast donated cuddly toys to them.

Treating Tricksters
MrBeast stunned an entire family when a child knocked on his door at Halloween and he gave them the whole house!

Restoring Hearing
After fixing up eyesight, MrBeast created a similar project and gave 1,000 hearing aids to deaf people!

Sky High Soccer Fans
A bunch of soccer obsessed street kids in Brazil were stunned when MrBeast flew them to a World Championship tournament, in Doha!

TOP FIVE

Coolest Collabs

FAMOUS FRIENDS
MrBeast has also been joined by special guests like talkshow host Jay Leno, comedian Pete Davidson, and celebrity chef Gordon Ramsey.

Celebs love appearing in MrBeast videos. Here are some of his most memorable buddy ups!

1

BTS

They may not be close pals but technically MrBeast has worked with the world's biggest boy band! In 2022, they collaborated with rapper Snoop Dogg and producer Benny Blanco on the song 'Bad Decisions.' Benny thought it would be cool if MrBeast got involved. So he pressed one key on a keyboard and officially made the song credits!

2

The Rock

MrBeast caught up with the WWE icon on the red carpet at the launch of Black Adam for a classic game of Rock, Paper, Scissors. They agreed that the loser would donate $100,000 to charity! Both went with paper first, followed by scissors, for two draws. Finally, The Rock won but insisted on donating anyway—which meant $200,000 going to Make-A-Wish, a children's charity.

Tom Brady

3

The number one quarterback in NFL history joined MrBeast on board a $300 million yacht in his '$1 vs $1,000,000,000 Yacht' video. The pair explored the boat and played a game of catch, and then set up some moving targets for Tom Brady to hit. These included Karl, who was driving a jetski and tried to catch the football (but missed!) and a moving drone, which was successfully knocked out of the sky.

Justin Timberlake

4

One of the 2000s' biggest stars appeared in the same video as Miranda Cosgrove. It compared living in a $1 house with a $139 million mansion! Justin had loads of fun exploring all the elegant parts of the deluxe home, like its own night club and T-Rex skeleton! It had twelve bedrooms, seventeen bathrooms and a perfect view of Los Angeles. Justin joked he'd buy it so long as it came with Nolan's shirt!

Miranda Cosgrove

5

MrBeast may have two Nickelodeon Kids' Choice Awards but *iCarly* star Miranda Cosgrove has won four! MrBeast and Miranda toured a $69 million tsunami-proof house, and got her to guess the value of the expensive artwork. The team had to promise not to touch the homeowner's super rare sound system, which had been built by the creator of the Walkman—one of the first gadgets for listening to music on the go!

MrBeast's Biggest Awards

As well as racking up monstrous subscriber numbers, MrBeast has earned some amazing awards on his rise to the top!

Breakout Creator

MrBeast's first major award came at the Streamy Awards in 2019. He beat Danny Gonzalez and LARRAY to win Breakout Creator! The award celebrates the person who burst onto the YouTube scene in the most spectacular way. MrBeast won for videos like 'I Opened The World's First Free Store'!

YouTuber of the Year

The Shorty Awards are all about celebrating the very best of social media. That put MrBeast in very famous company when he grabbed this trophy in 2020! Rebel Wilson won Best Celebrity, Zendaya was named Best Actor, and Greta Thunberg was awarded the prize for Best in Activism. Other nominees included Demi Lovato and Beyonce!

The first Streamy Award that MrBeast won, in 2020, before he won another three times in a row.

Creator of the Year

MrBeast was first nominated for this Streamy Award in 2019 but missed out to influencer Tana Mongeau. Since then, he's triumphed! He won it four years in a row, from 2020 to 2023. For that last one, he was up against Jay Shetty, Alix Earle, and Prime king Logan Paul. But they still couldn't loosen his grip on the prize!

MrBeast holding his Shorty Award, which is shaped like a whale's tail, after winning YouTuber of the Year.

100% UNOFFICIAL

Other Nominations

MrBeast is yet to win these ones, but has been shortlisted for them. You can be sure he'll snap them up eventually!

Ensemble Cast, Streamy Awards

Favorite Male Social Star, Kids' Choice Awards

Creator Product, Streamy Awards

Social Impact Campaign, Streamy Awards

MrBeast working with Mark Rober and Kris for Team Seas, which won him a Social Good Award.

The Gold YouTube Creator Award, which MrBeast won when he hit 1 million followers.

Social Good

The 2020 Streamy Awards were a beastly breakthrough and not just for MrBeast's Creator of the Year prize. He also scored the Live Special Award for a $250,000 Rock, Paper, Scissors tournament. And won Social Good Awards for Team Trees philanthropy and his Feeding America food drive! Team Seas earned him another Social Good prize in 2022.

Red Diamond Creator Award

This was actually MrBeast's fifth YouTube Creator Award for incredible subscriber numbers. He got the Silver Award at 100,000, then Gold for 1 million. 10 million earned him the Diamond Award, then the Ruby Award arrived at 50 million. Finally, at 100 million, he won the Red Diamond Award. It's a massive glass play button!

Favorite Male Creator

The Nickelodeon Kids' Choice Awards have been running since 1988. That made 2023 the 36th year! MrBeast fought off Austin Creed, AKA WWE wrestler Xavier Woods, to win Favorite Male Creator. It was the second year running that MrBeast nabbed this title!

Red Diamond Winners

Only eight influencers or companies have earned the Red Diamond button. They are:

MrBeast
PewDiePie
T-Series
CoComelon
Like Nastya
Vlad and Niki
SET India
WWE

MrBeast posed on the red carpet before winning Favorite Male Creator at the Nickelodeon Kids' Choice Awards.

ALL ABOUT Feastables

Everyone wants MrBeast's chocolate and cookies! Here's the tale of how Feastables came to be so big ...

Global Feast

To begin with, Feastables could only be found in USA supermarket Walmart. The bars and cookies gradually spread to other shops, too. The UK was first—Asda and Spar started stocking Feastables in 2023. They're also now available in Canada, Australia, New Zealand, and South Africa!

Choc and Awe

MrBeast Bars were first announced in January 2022, to launch the Feastables range. The full selection includes chocolate bars, snack bars, cookies, and gummy sweets known as Karl Gummies!

In February 2024, MrBeast posted a dramatic announcement video, telling the world that he had made Feastables even better!

Pack of Nutz

The first three Feastables flavors were Original, Almond, and Quinoa Crunch. That last one was later replaced with Milk Crunch. Deez Nutz also became a super popular flavor. However, it had to have its name changed for legal reasons. It's now called Peanut Butter. Much more simple!

Hard to Find

Feastables are so popular that fans have sometimes struggled to find them. MrBeast even apologized for the shortages! He wrote on X (formerly Twitter), "I'm doing everything I can to get some more chocolate factories up and running! Sorry for not being able to buy it right now."

A shelf of tasty treats for Feastables fans (and MrBeast fans) to enjoy.

100% UNOFFICIAL

Fans have a huge choice of different Feastables to choose from in this well-stocked store.

Hidden Prizes

MrBeast relaunched Feastables with an improved recipe in February 2024. To celebrate the improved candy, he gave away $10,000 every day for thirty days. All fans had to do to be in with a chance of winning was scan a QR code on the wrapper!

In the video 'Buy Feastables, Win $10,000', MrBeast handed one very lucky shopper a suitcase full of cash!

Beastly Halloween

Halloween 2022 brought a special spooky snack. MrBeast teamed up with streamer Corpse Husband. They launched a cookies-and-creme Corpse Feastables Bar! It had a white chocolate base and was bright (and blood) red! You could only order it through the Feastables website and naturally it sold out!

One Stop Pop-ups

In November 2023, MrBeast created a Feastables pop-up shop in New York City! It was open for three days. Fans could buy merch and try free coffee or iced chocolate. Some got to enter challenges for cash prizes. At the end, everyone got a goody bag. Inside was a hat, cup, and four chocolate bars!

Hornet Food

Feastables is the official sponsor of NBA team the Charlotte Hornets. That means they have the snazzy logo on their jerseys for every game!

TOP FIVE

Travel Tales

He lives in the USA but many of MrBeast's best videos have been filmed away from home.

By day four, the team was tired of the camping food and tried fishing for something new to eat.

7 Days Stranded On An Island

The gang joined MrBeast on an island that's been deserted for 250 years! The group had to build a shelter and catch food while avoiding hazards, like the most dangerous tree on Earth! Other problems included bug bites, sunburn, and storm water pooling on the roof of their shelter. But they stuck it out for a whole week!

$1 vs $250,000 Vacation

The Beast Gang started out in a $1 shack, with a bed and mattress surrounded by sand! Much better was a $50,000 trip to Paris, where they got the Eiffel Tower all to themselves. As for the biggest of the lot: that took them to Tokyo. They stayed in Japan's most expensive hotel, ate in a robot restaurant, and had samurai lessons!

MrBeast took samurai lessons—including katana classes—while in Japan on the $250,000 vacation.

100% UNOFFICIAL

3 Surviving 24 Hours Straight In The Bermuda Triangle

The Bermuda Triangle is a mysterious area in the Caribbean. Over 100 planes and ships have disappeared inside it! So naturally, MrBeast took the gang there for twenty-four hours. Kris and Chandler struggled badly with seasickness but the danger they feared never materialized. In fact, the gang had fun on jet skis and floats, before returning to dry land in Miami.

Marcus, Jake the Viking, Chandler, and Kris fought to stay on the float and win $2,000.

4 I Survived 50 Hours In Antarctica

Minecraft influencers Dream and GeorgeNotFound joined MrBeast's crew in the coldest place on the planet! They were immediately greeted by a blizzard, then had to deal with twenty-four-hour daylight, sickness, and a strange new way to use the toilet. To pee in Antarctica, you have to go in a bottle then hang onto it until you find a specific drop-off point on the map!

The team's first job when they arrived, was to set up camp and protect their tents with an ice wall.

5 Seven Days Stranded At Sea

"How much longer?" asked Kris during this one ... after less than seven seconds! The gang were on a raft in the middle of the ocean and had to build a shelter, but it was three days before they managed to cook a hot meal! Drama arrived overnight on day four, as a wild storm brought lightning, wind, and twenty hours of non-stop rain.

Immediately after they were dropped off, MrBeast and his friends rushed to make a shelter.

MrBeast, Record Breaker

MrBeast has smashed numerous records over the years—and amazingly Chandler has grabbed a couple, too!

MrBeast and his team showed the contestants to the sleeping area, which was decorated exactly like the TV show.

X-treme Reposts

In January 2024, MrBeast gave away $250,000 via a simple X post: "I'm gonna give 10 random people that repost this and follow me $25,000 for fun." It soon became the most reposted post in the site's history, with 3.3 million shares!

Tampa Yay

MrBeast made NFL history when he led the Tampa Bay Buccaneers out for a game. The official video of him running on to the field became the most popular post in the team's history, with 701,000 Instagram likes! Sadly, they lost the game 13-16.

Squids In

As well as being MrBeast's most-watched video, '$456,000 Squid Game In Real Life' shattered three YouTube records. It got 42.6 million views in one day, which is the record for a non-music/trailer/rewind video. It scored the most subscribers in one day: 1.4 million. And it was the fastest non-music video to reach 100 million views in less than four days.

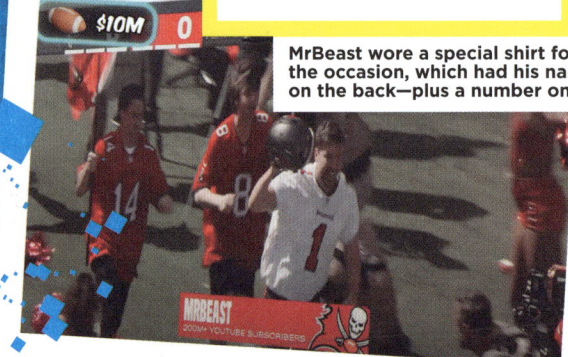

MrBeast wore a special shirt for the occasion, which had his name on the back—plus a number one!

100% UNOFFICIAL

YouTube Billionaire

MrBeast got one of his shorts to pass 1 billion YouTube views in November 2023—then repeated the milestone a few days later! 'Would You Fly To Paris For A Baguette' was first to hit 1 billion views, followed soon after by 'Giving iPhones Instead Of Candy On Halloween.'

The very lucky guest star in MrBeast's first video to hit 1 billion views, who was flown to Paris.

Biggest Burger

MrBeast holds the Guinness World Record for 'Largest Vegetarian Burger in the World'! It was 0.87m tall and took forty-three people to prepare. The top bun alone weighed roughly the same as the average grizzly bear!

Cam The Man

Former NFL quarterback Cam Newton broke three Guinness World Records with the help of the Beast Gang! While MrBeast might laugh at Chandler for his antics, he shared two of the records with him—including 'Most One Handed Catches In A Minute'!

Record Collector

Along with the largest veggie burger, MrBeast owns three other Guinness World Records. They are 'Highest-earning YouTube contributor (current),' 'Most Subscribers for an Individual Male on YouTube,' and 'First Person to Reach 1 Million Followers on Threads.'

ALL ABOUT Video Games

MrBeast is a dedicated gamer—as you'll know if you've watched MrBeast Gaming! These are just some of his faves …

Among Us

This brilliant game is like the TV show *The Traitors*. Players are split between Crewmates and Impostors. Crewmates have to hunt all the Impostors, or the enemy team wins! Kris, Chandler, and Karl all feature in *Among Us* videos with MrBeast—along with other YouTubers, such as Dream, Georgenotfound, and Sapnap.

League of Legends

What's MrBeast's favorite game ever? "Definitely *League of Legends*," he told fans in a YouTube video. "The best video game ever created is *League*. I don't care what you say!" It's an online battle arena, where two teams of five face off. Despite coming out in 2009, it still has a huge following!

In *Among Us*, gamers can play with either small or big groups online, between 4 and 15 people!

MrBeast's favorite game, *League of Legends*, is one of the biggest eSports games.

100% UNOFFICIAL

Minecraft

The blocky world builder is a big focus of the MrBeast Games channel. Its top five most-watched videos are all from *Minecraft*. They include 'If You Build A House, I'll Pay For It.' 100 players had an hour to build the coolest home in the game. MrBeast then bought the winner, SaveMrSquishy, a house in real life!

MrBeast watched 100 players build houses in *Minecraft*, before he chose the winner.

Fortnite

The Beast Gang are big fans of this customizable shooter. So naturally, MrBeast has two skins that pop up in the Item Shop! His normal skin, which looks just like him, was added as part of the MrBeast Set. It also contains treats like the Beast Claw pickaxe. His second skin was part of the *Lego Fortnite* update. It recreates him in brick form!

The classic MrBeast *Fortnite* skin and the helmet version, which is designed to look like his logo.

Stumble Guys

MrBeast loves this battle royale so much, he teamed up with the creators to appear in the game! His warehouse HQ is recreated as a race map. It cleverly takes inspiration from his real videos. There are Feastables references—and a chocolate river based on 'I Recreated Willy Wonka's Chocolate Factory'!

MrBeast as Willy Wonka in *Stumble Guys*, which contains beast characters in MrBeast merch.

... And One He's Less Fond Of

One of MrBeast's funniest videos is 'Playing The Worst Rated Video Game.' He, Kris, Chandler, and Karl try *Block Warriors*—the lowest-rated game on Steam! They wander round the blocky world trying different stuff, like mashing every button on the keyboard. MrBeast said he wouldn't recommend it, but Kris reckoned, "it was enjoyable!"

TOP FIVE

Crazy Challenges

Could you count non-stop for 40 hours, or defend a tank from missiles? Then you're in the right place!

1. I Counted To 100,000

The video that kickstarted MrBeast's rise to fame! It took nearly forty hours, although the video was edited down to twenty-four. That still means it would take you all day to watch it! Kris entered the room at number 36,000 to try to distract him. The last hour was agony, as MrBeast tried to finish the challenge without falling asleep!

MrBeast had to wrap up warm for this chilly challenge! He also kept moving around in circles.

2. I Survived 24 Hours Straight In Ice

This must be the coldest MrBeast challenge ever. He was encased in a small ice house filled with ice sculptures. Even the toilet seat was made of ice! The challenge got so painful, a medic had to check on MrBeast every thirty minutes. The punishment for losing was being covered in syrup and feathers. MrBeast survived, so Chandler, Kris, Karl, and Tyler became human birds instead!

Snapshots of the 24-hour-long video that made MrBeast go viral for the first time.

100% UNOFFICIAL

3

Lamborghini vs World's Largest Shredder

If you love cars, this clip is torture! Seeing a beautiful red Lamborghini being torn to bits was just one of the brain-breaking experiments in this video. The gang also built the world's largest domino, then used it to completely flatten a supermarket! And they blew up a giant *Minecraft* Creeper and launched an explosive carriage off the end of a rollercoaster!

As well as this red Lamborghini, they also shredded a piano, a crate of Coca Cola bottles, and a Hershey's vending machine.

Blake Manning took MrBeast up on his challenge to protect this giant pile of cash—using MrBeast's credit card to buy protection!

4

Protect $500,000 Then Keep It

Can TikToker Blake Manning protect a $500,000 money pile from five tanks launching missiles? Using MrBeast's credit card, Blake purchased giant crates to go over the money and trucks to park in front of it. The money survived the initial missiles and a bomb attack too, but was later burned and ruined by flaming cars. Poor Blake!

5

Protect The Lamborghini, Keep It!

Blake returned for one final shot at a big win. This time, the prize was a Lamborghini! Again, he was given MrBeast's credit card to build up protection. That included a water truck, cinder blocks, and junk cars. MrBeast then unleashed 10,000 bullets. The car survived those and flaming vehicles but how about a 35mph train? At last, Blake got his victory, plus $100,000 in cash!

While MrBeast and Blake stayed with the Lamborghini, Karl gave updates on the train's speed.

MrBeast In Numbers

All the important figures, stats, and digits that explain MrBeast's rise!

84,664 — The number of comments on '7 Days Stranded On An Island' in the first 24 hours after it was uploaded!

500,000,000 — In September 2023, '$456,000 Squid Game In Real Life' became MrBeast's first video to beat this incredible number of views!

10 — The number of subscribers MrBeast had on his 13th birthday. Ten years later, it had risen to 61.6 million!

95,000,000 — MrBeast's total TikTok followers in May 2024. Only Khaby Lame and Charli D'Amelio have more!

250,000 — MrBeast's average number of new subscribers per day, in June 2024!

February 19th 2012 — The date MrBeast's main channel was created on YouTube.

100% UNOFFICIAL

DAY 70

12,000
Hours of footage recorded for 'Survive 100 Days Trapped, Win $500,000.' The two contestants lasted 100 days and decided to split the prize!

70.1%
The percentage of people who said they'd vote for MrBeast if he ran for president of the USA! As voted for in a poll on X.

41%
Percentage of MrBeast viewers aged between twenty and thirty, according to a poll he posted on X. 39.7% are aged between ten and twenty!

10,000
The number of subscribers MrBeast had when his mom discovered he was a YouTuber!

1,111
Number of lottery tickets MrBeast bought to celebrate 111,111,111 subscribers!

$1,300,000
Total cost of Feastables given away when MrBeast made all his chocolate bars free for ten minutes on X!

197
Number of competitors in the 'Every Country On Earth Fights For $250,000!' video.

1%
Percentage of the human population that watches a MrBeast video once it's uploaded!

1/4
MrBeast told content creator Marques Brownlee that one out of every four videos he makes gets scrapped because it just doesn't work!

ALL ABOUT MrBeast's Hometown

Welcome to Greenville, North Carolina. MrBeast's hometown has been completely transformed by his supersonic rise!

Jimmy Wonka

Many of MrBeast's videos are filmed on the outskirts of Greenville. 'I Built Willy Wonka's Chocolate Factory' was shot there. So were the experiments from 'Lamborghini vs World's Largest Shredder'.

Big Bangs

MrBeast's explosions have become a normal part of living in Greenville. Local officials send out "planned pyrotechnics" emails to residents and use Facebook to ask them not to call the police!

Booming Business

The town's biggest businesses are pharmaceuticals, forklifts, and YouTube. But the last one of those is down to one person alone! Wonder who that could be?

Job Offers

MrBeast is constantly searching for artists, cleaners, and builders. He even placed a job ad for construction workers who have experience in putting up a haunted house!

It's a Dog's Life

MrBeast's favorite restaurant, Sup Dogs, is in the north east of town. He's been going there since way before he was famous. In 'Ordering Water Then Tipping $30,000', MrBeast gave one of the waitresses $10,000!

100% UNOFFICIAL

College City

Greenville is also home to East Carolina University. It's been open since 1907 and has 28,000 students. Sports fans are catered for by its own American football team, the ECU Pirates. Their stadium can hold 51,000 supporters!

Expensive Tastes

MrBeast's HQ is in Greenville and has around 250 employees. The building is estimated to have cost him $14.1 million. $2.9 million of that was on tech like computers, cameras, and lighting!

The Power Of Four

MrBeast's first house cost $318,000. It has four bathrooms and four bedrooms. He's also bought the four nearest ones to make his own cul-de-sac for friends and family.

Studio Sleeper

Most of the filming at HQ is done in Studio C. It's around 50,000 square feet in size. MrBeast has an apartment there, with a bed, fridge, and weightlifting bench. He once told a podcast that he was so busy, he'd only left once in twenty days!

Famous Locals

The city has a population of 87,500, making it the 12th biggest in North Carolina. It was founded in 1771 and originally called Martinsborough. Famous actress Sandra Bullock went to university in Greenville and BMX boss Josh Harrington was born there!

TOP FIVE
Spooky Scares

Not all MrBeast videos are for the faint hearted. These will make you grateful for a good night's sleep.

1. I Spent 50 Hours In Solitary Confinement

Imagine spending over two days in a single room. That's what MrBeast did for this one! He only had the basics, like a bed and a toilet. Oh, and a TV but it was controlled by Kris! If MrBeast survived all 50 hours, the gang got slimed, so they tried various tactics to force him out. Like playing an iPhone alarm for three hours and stealing his bedding!

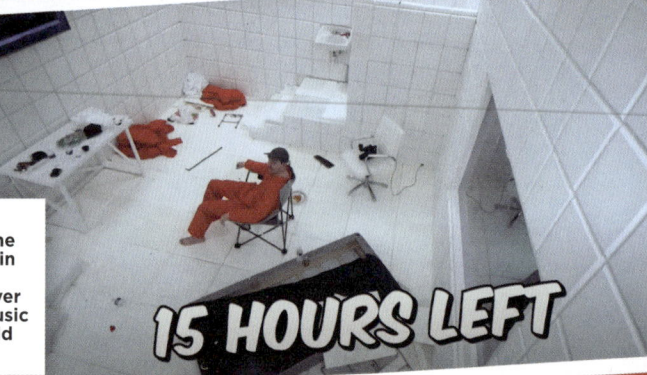

MrBeast had very little in the cell to entertain himself with, except whatever videos and music the gang would play for him.

2. I Spent 50 Hours Buried Alive

MrBeast spent fifty hours in a coffin, covered by layers of soil. He had water, air conditioning, and a two way-radio to speak to his crew. However, they were also there to make it harder for him and taser him if he escaped early! At the end, MrBeast was so happy, he cried!

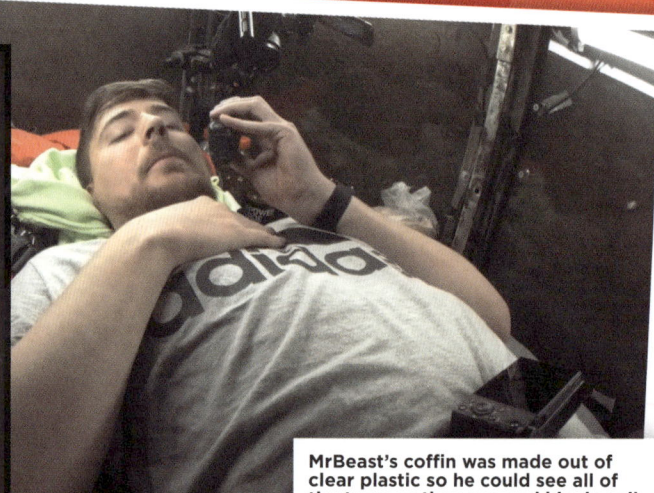

MrBeast's coffin was made out of clear plastic so he could see all of the team as they covered him in soil. The gang then sat above the soil and communicated via walkie talkie.

100% UNOFFICIAL

Unlike other challenges, the team was told at the beginning that they couldn't make any deals.

3 I Spent 24 Hours Straight In Insane Asylum

The Beast Gang split into two teams for this challenge: Kris and Ethan vs Chandler and Zero. Whoever survived longest was supposed to win $10,000. All the contestants were in straightjackets with their arms wrapped up—and had to deal with flickering lights. Chandler and Kris both had to quit for medical reasons, so one member of each team, Ethan and Zero, split the money instead!

4 I Spent 24 Hours Straight In Prison

MrBeast, Chandler, Kris, and Garrett had to spend a full day and night behind bars! They were spread across two bunk beds in one cell and quickly got bored. Things worsened when Chandler's farts made the room smell, as Kris put it, "like butt cakes!" The crew eventually escaped with the help of a birthday cake for Garrett, which had sneaky tools hidden inside!

The team was escorted to a real-life cell—with barred gates—by guards and locked in.

5 24 Hours In The Most Haunted Place On Earth

The gang stayed over inside the Ohio State Penitentiary—a vast and spooky prison. They went ghost hunting with flashlights, walkie talkies, and a special detector for electromagnetic activity! Despite MrBeast saying he doesn't believe in ghosts, there really were some scary moments. Tareq got so frightened that he screamed and sprinted back to base camp while still filming!

Ignoring all the rules of horror movies, the team split up and kept in touch with walkie talkies.

MrBeast's Movie Moments

He's mastered YouTube. He's conquered chocolate and cookies. Now MrBeast is crossing over into Hollywood!

Teenage Mutant Ninja Turtles: Mutant Mayhem

MrBeast's first voice acting role was a part in *Mutant Mayhem*! He plays a minor character called Times Square Guy. During a flashback sequence, he taps Splinter on the ear, figuring that the turtles' sensei is a human wearing a costume. When he realizes Splinter is a real rat, he screams and runs away!

Raphael, Leonardo, Donatello, and Michelangelo in *Teenage Mutant Ninja Turtles: Mutant Mayhem*.

The movie poster for *Under the Boardwalk*, where MrBeast played a crab living in a hot sauce bottle.

Under The Boardwalk

Kids' movie *Under The Boardwalk* is a musical comedy featuring loads of catchy tunes. It follows a bunch of hermit crabs who live on New Jersey beach. Keke Palmer and Michael Cera play the main roles, but MrBeast has a small part, too! He plays the Hot Sauce Crab. This smiley crustacean drags around a bottle of hot sauce on his back!

100% UNOFFICIAL

Kung Fu Panda 4

MrBeast clearly enjoys playing animals on the big screen. This time, he's Panda Pig! You've guessed it—that means he's half panda, half pig, with a black-and-white face but big snout. He only has one line, but it's an important one: "Skadoosh!" MrBeast auditioned for the role by reciting that word on a video call with Jack Black!

Po and Shifu from Kung Fu Panda 4, voiced by Jack Black and Dustin Hoffman.

Dune Part 2

While there wasn't an actual part for MrBeast in this one, he still produced a cool crossover. He co-hosted a tournament of the board game Dune Imperium—and as part of it, contestants got a sneak preview of the new movie. MrBeast won the game, to claim $10,000!

The final table in the Dune Imperium challenge, where MrBeast won $10,000.

ALL ABOUT Beast Gang Gross-Outs

MrBeast loves to gross out the Beast Gang! These are some yuck-tastic highlights ...

Barf-worthy Breakfast

Could you sit in your breakfast for nearly a day? Four challengers did in 'World's Largest Bowl of Cereal!' It was 2,000 gallons in size. Inside was water, powdered milk, and expired Frosted Flakes and Cap'n Crunch cereal. The winner survived twenty hours, to claim $10,000. MrBeast said they smelled of "urine and milk.' Ewww!

Goo-Filled House

MrBeast's Team Trees buddy Mark Rober won two world records involving elephant toothpaste. So MrBeast used some to ruin his brother CJBro's house. Literally every room was coated in green foam! Thankfully, he saw the funny side, especially when MrBeast bought him a plush new home!

Karl enjoyed jumping onto one of the foam covered beds and splashing green goo everywhere!

A Day in Slime

MrBeast promised that if he failed to spend twenty-four hours in a tank of slime, he would give Jake The Viking $100,000! He was wearing a wetsuit but it was still super cold. MrBeast did manage to get a couple of hours' sleep by propping a pillow on a blow-up mattress. By the end, even though it was green slime, his fingers had turned blue!

Despite swimming in green slime, MrBeast still managed to take a nap with the help of an air mattress.

Green Marathon

In 'Last To Leave Slime Pit Wins $20,000,' it was the Beast Gang's turn to try to survive in a tank of the green stuff. There was a surprise contestant, too. Chandler's dad! The audience loved him. While pal Garrett Ronalds lasted longest, Chandler's dad survived more than eleven hours, and finished second!

Garrett, Chandler's dad, Chandler, and Ethan tried out the same slime challenge as MrBeast.

$20,000 of Sweat!

'Last To Stop Running Wins $20,000' is the sweatiest video MrBeast has ever made! Chandler, Marcus, and Kris were joined by their friend Ty. They had to stay on treadmills for as long as possible and inevitably ended up completely drenched! Ty won the challenge after running thirteen miles.

To motivate his friends, MrBeast played videos on the green screen of dinosaurs chasing them.

Human Soup

MrBeast's friends get dunked in food a lot! In 'Last To Leave Ramen Noodle Pool Wins $20,000,' Chandler went up against his family. His sisters Hannah and Cassidy, and brother Zach joined him in the pool and his dad was referee! His sisters shared gross secrets, like when he pooed all over the bathroom walls! Chandler was out first, while Cassidy won.

Chandler and his family sharing a ramen noodle hot tub, as well as some family secrets!

100% UNOFFICIAL

TOP FIVE
Greatest Giveaways

MrBeast videos are often life-changing for those who appear in them. These ones all created some truly emotional memories!

1. Press This Button To Win $100,000

MrBeast prepared a giant red button, which dished out a random punishment when one of his pals pressed it. Except for one lucky gang member, who got $100,000 to give to his mom or sister! Kris kicked things off by having to wear pants filled with mayonnaise, while Chandler had to build a six-year-old *Minecraft* LEGO set. Karl (and his sister) eventually won!

Chandler helped this very lucky shopper win over $3,000 of gaming consoles and accessories.

One of the grossest challenges in this video was Kris wearing pants filled with mayonnaise.

2. Anything You Can Fit In The Circle I'll Pay For

MrBeast placed red circles on the floors of stores and told shoppers he'd pay for anything they could fit inside. If they touched the red tape, they got nothing! One young gamer won a bundle of gaming consoles. The best bit was when they helped out a soup kitchen. Its manager filled the circle with $6,000 worth of food and water, before MrBeast donated a cheque for an extra $20,000!

44

100% UNOFFICIAL

3 | I Gave People 1 Million Dollars But Only One Minute To Spend It

The first family to take on this challenge managed multiple TVs, a load of Funko Pop figures, and $13,000 in gift cards. That was clever, as it meant they could go back to spend it later! One lucky winner dropped $60,990 in a jewelry store. School teacher Jordan got bonus time to gather goodies for her students and a suitcase with $10,000 in cash for herself!

MrBeast paid for $13,000 in gift cards for this very smart (and lucky) winner!

MrBeast told Joey that the house was actually for him, and then gave him a tour around his new home.

4 | I Ordered Pizza And Tipped The House

Domino's delivery guy Joey arrived at MrBeast's new house with a fresh pepperoni pizza and was asked to help carry in furniture for some extra cash. Throughout the day, MrBeast found out his background and filled the house with dog food and toys for his daughter. Fourteen hours later, Joey discovered the house was really for him and cried tears of joy!

5 | Every Country On Earth Fights For $250,000

MrBeast flew a person from every single country to the USA, where they all competed for a $250,000 gold medal! Contestants battled at running, gymnastics, archery, and fencing. Slovenia and Libya faced one another in a final penalty shootout! Libya saved Slovenia's penalty, then slammed the ball into the top corner—before falling to his knees in celebration!

The contestants sized each other up before the dramatic penultimate challenge of fencing on a bridge.

At Home With MrBeast

These are a few of the ways MrBeast spends his time when he isn't making YouTube videos ...

Keeping Fit

MrBeast can't exactly go for a run around his hometown. He's so famous, he'd be mobbed with every footstep! Instead, he works out by doing 12,500 steps every day. He gets his health advice from Paraskevas Kaltsas—another content creator, who is also a personal trainer!

Video Gaming

Bet you'd already guessed this one! MrBeast's favorite game is *League of Legends*. But given that he has his own gaming channel, there are plenty of others he likes too. *Minecraft*, *Fortnite*, and *Among Us* are some of the most famous.

100% UNOFFICIAL

Hanging With The Gang

MrBeast really is close friends with the crew in real life. Chandler and Kris were both born and raised in his hometown of Greenville and still live there today!

Watching Anime

Anime is a style of Japanese cartoon. MrBeast is a fan and especially loved a grown-up series called *Death Note*. It's about a book where if you write the person's name in it, they die!

Saving Dollars

MrBeast might have plenty of cash, but he thinks carefully about spending it. "I went through that phase where I bought nice clothes and I drove an i8, but I don't like attention," he told PayPal Honey. "At the moment, I feel like I live a very un-materialistic life." In case you're wondering, the i8 is a super speedy BMW car!

Listening to Audiobooks

MrBeast loves listening to audiobooks! He posted on X that *The 7 Habits of Highly Effective People* by Stephen R. Cowey is "the best book ever." He also loved Scott Galloway's *The Four*. That one is about how Amazon, Apple, Facebook, and Google took over the world!

47

ALL ABOUT
Team Trees & Team Seas

MrBeast's biggest philanthropy projects have made a huge difference to the environment. They're called Team Trees and Team Seas …

Team Trees

Every year, trees around the world are chopped down so the land can be used. This process is called deforestation. MrBeast teamed up with fellow influencer Mark Rober, to do the opposite! They announced Team Trees in October 2019. Its aim was raising $20 million for 20 million trees. That target was hit before the end of the year!

Team Trees managed to raise $20 million to put toward planting new trees in less than a year.

Team Seas

MrBeast's second project with Mark Rober focused on removing junk from the oceans. Their target this time was to raise $30 million. That could then be used to remove 30 million pounds' worth of rubbish from our seas. By March 2024, they'd soared past that target, with $33.6 million raised!

Clever Fan

The original idea for Team Trees came from a fan! A user called vdnx posted an image of Lisa Simpson on reddit in May 2019. On a whiteboard behind Lisa, they had written: "Petition for MrBeast to plant 20 million trees for [a] 20 million subscribers special and single handedly save Earth." It got 56,000 likes and MrBeast's attention!

100% UNOFFICIAL

Worldwide Wonder

Team Trees has completed its original goal of 20 million trees planted. The project spanned the globe, too! More than one million trees went to the nation of Haiti. The beautiful Michigan State Forests in the USA were blessed with 2.2 million fresh trees. The UK got new trees too, with 270,000 planted in the Mersey Forest, near Liverpool!

Busy Beach Trip

MrBeast and Mark Rober made a special visit to the Dominican Republic to kickstart Team Seas. They demonstrated the three different areas that the campaign focuses on. Rubbish has to be cleared from beaches, rivers, and oceans to improve the environment! They filmed their work, too. You can see it in the video 'I Cleaned The World's Dirtiest Beach.'

The River Forest, near Liverpool in the UK was one of the areas that Team Trees helped.

MrBeast and Team Seas helped clean up the trash from the beach and surrounding areas in Santo Domingo.

Halfway Finished

While both Team Trees and Team Seas quickly hit their financial targets, it takes a long time to carry out the work. In May 2023, MrBeast announced that Team Seas was halfway towards its goal. 112,000 volunteers had cleared 15.1 million pounds of waste in 63 countries.

TOP FIVE

Toy Stories

You're never too old to play with LEGO! While MrBeast loves to build his videos around it, other childhood faves get a mention, too ...

MrBeast and Kris started piling the prizes up, and then Kris climbed inside the giant pile at the end!

1 I Put 10 Million LEGOs In Friend's House

MrBeast's pals Bailey and Jake The Viking agreed to lend him their house for a day, they thought he would be filling the house with gifts. Those gifts turned out to be 10 million LEGO bricks! Bailey's room was covered in sticky notes. Bailey and Jake were shocked but did get real presents too: mini vehicles with cash in the boot.

2 I Won Every Prize At A Theme Park

The Beast Gang tried to grab every possible prize at a theme park. Basketball, Whac-A-Mole, and Ring Toss were just three of the games the crew won, but they couldn't complete a tough game where they hung off a bar for ninety seconds. They won such a huge stack of toys that Kris joked she was going to live in the pile then disappeared underneath it!

The team placed boxes under the LEGOS, making it look even more packed full of bricks.

100% UNOFFICIAL

As they built the towers higher, the team had to wear safety gear, like hard hats, to use the cranes.

3
Giant Monopoly Game With Real Money

Monopoly is way more fun when you're playing for cash! Four contestants played on an oversized board, using real dollars instead of *Monopoly* notes! The winner got to keep the real value of all their hotels and properties, meaning a cool $10,400 for victor Logan. Kind as always, MrBeast gave the three defeated players $2,000 each, too!

4
I Built The World's Largest LEGO Tower

This challenge sounded simple before the addition of trucks, cranes, and bowling balls! Team Kris and Team Chandler got to attack one another's towers and use proper machinery to make their creations even taller. Incredibly, Chandler's team won by one inch but he had to make do with just a handful of cash after leaving early!

5
I Put 100 Million Orbeez In My Friend's Backyard

Orbeez are magical beads that grow when you add water. The plan here was to take 100 boxes, each containing one million Orbeez, spread them over a backyard then wait for it to rain. Kris got buried under a massive pile, while other challenges included swimming in Orbeez and Orbeez baseball!

Each of the contestants would walk around the board with their houses, hotels, and money—till lucky Logan won the game!

Jake the Viking had to help pull Kris out from under the Orbeez in the swimming pool!

MrBeast's Abandoned City

Behind the scenes of the sunny Croatian beach resort made famous by a MrBeast video …

The Grand Hotel in Kupari is one of the buildings that the team explored in this challenge.

Abandoned Treasures (Sort Of!)

Here are just some of the weird and wonderful items the gang found during their week in Kupari …

Old mattress (Chandler)
Cute cat (Everyone)
Working bike (Kris)
Shelves (Mark & MrBeast)
Table (MrBeast)
Carpet (Mark & MrBeast)
Chair (Mark)
Fake TV (MrBeast)
Wallpaper (Mark & MrBeast)
Kayak (Mark & MrBeast)
Football (Kris)

A Week Away

'I Survived 7 Days In An Abandoned City' brought fame to Kupari in Croatia. MrBeast, Chandler, and Kris were joined by Team Trees teammate Mark Rober. They explored a popular resort that had been destroyed by war. Chandler and Kris had to leave halfway through the challenge, after Mark dropped half the group's water off a roof! But he and MrBeast made it to the end.

On the second day, the team found a better shelter to spend the night but had to go back to their old spot to pick up all their camping gear.

100% UNOFFICIAL

Seven Sisters

The gang explored two crumbling hotels and discovered a disused sports court and swimming pool. But you could see even more buildings in the background. That's because there are actually seven abandoned hotels in Kupari! They're called the Grand, Goričina I, Goričina II, Kupari, Pelegrin, Mladost, and Galeb.

Kupari is also known as "the bay of dead hotels," as there are so many abandoned resorts.

Happier History

The Grand Hotel opened in 1923. A bunch more hotels popped up in the 1960s, as the bay became popular for members of the Yugoslav army and their families. 4,500 people could stay there at once! In 1991, a war between Croatia and Yugoslavia saw Kupari attacked from the sea. In the 2000s it was finally abandoned.

Public Transport

Although it looked like the only people around were the gang and their cameraman, there are still people living in Kupari. The city has an official population of 950! You can actually get there easily—and not just by helicopter. It's around a 15-minute drive from the city Dubrovnik and there's even a bus that stops there. Tourists love to stop for a sunbathe!

Famous Visitor

Miley Cyrus' little sister Noah Cyrus filmed a music video in Kupari! It was for the song 'All Fall Down,' which she made with Norwegian DJ Alan Walker. Almost all of the music video was filmed around the Hotel Goricina. Recognize it? That's because MrBeast spent most of his time there in his video, too!

ALL ABOUT Sports

MrBeast loves to get involved in sports. Whether that's watching it, funding it, or even playing it!

Missing Messi

MrBeast made a surprise appearance watching soccer when Inter Miami played CF Montreal in February 2024. Sadly, he didn't bring them luck on the day. Miami were missing legendary striker Lionel Messi. MrBeast got to celebrate goals from Leonardo Campana and Jordi Alba. But Montreal gathered themselves to grab a shock 3-2 win!

MrBeast wore an Inter Miami jersey when he went to watch the match against CF Montreal, it has Lionel Messi's name on the back!

Ultimate Fighter

Logan Paul crossed over to the sports entertainment world by coming WWE's United States Champion. MrBeast hasn't gone that far but did appear at UFC 299 alongside Logan and Sidemen star KSI! They watched bantamweight champ Sean O'Malley successfully defending his belt against Ecuadorian favorite Marlon Vera.

MrBeast attended UFC 299 but as a spectator not a fighter in the ring!

100% UNOFFICIAL

The new Charlotte Hornets jerseys feature MrBeast's logo on the top left corner.

Side Project

Sidemen are known to be really good soccer players. For a charity match in the summer of 2023, they brought in MrBeast to play alongside them! Former Premier League referee Mark Clattenburg was the ref and they played at a stadium in London. Sidemen won 8-5 but it wasn't all good news. MrBeast suffered a knee injury after a hard tackle from iShowSpeed!

To help promote the game for charity, MrBeast posed for photos in his Sidemen FC jersey.

Honorary Hornet

MrBeast is now part of the basketball world, after Feastables sponsored the Charlotte Hornets! Both their home and away jerseys have a Feastables logo on them. "I love basketball so it only makes sense for Feastables's first sponsorship to be with my home team," MrBeast announced on X.

Buc For A Day

For his '$1 vs $10,000,000 Job' video, MrBeast got to be an NFL player for a day. Two, actually! He signed a one year contract for $10 million—but agreed it would only last forty-eight hours and he wouldn't receive any real money. He practiced with the team, did a press conference, and led them on to the field for their clash with the Atlanta Falcons!

MrBeast got to lead the Tampa Bay NFL team out on to the field ahead of their game with the Falcons.

TOP FIVE
Guests & Rivals

MrBeast has crossed paths with other famous content creators over the years. This is what unfolded when he did!

Bella Poarch played in a giant game of tag, hide-and-seek, and Where's Karl? in MrBeast's influencer tournament.

1
PewDiePie
Felix Kjellberg is the most influential YouTuber ever, with over 29 billion views! 'Saying PewDiePie 100,000 Times' was one of MrBeast's breakthrough videos. MrBeast also supported PewDiePie in his subscriber race against Indian music label T-Series. The powerful pair finally met up for real in '$1 vs $250,000 Vacation.'

PewDiePie traveled to Japan to visit the theme park Fuji-Q Highland with MrBeast on his $250,000 vacation.

2
Bella Poarch
Bella was one of fifteen contenders in a legendary influencer tournament hosted by MrBeast. She was up against the likes of Logan Paul and ZHC to win $1 million! Challenges included searching for the real Karl in a stadium full of cardboard Karl cut-outs! Bella was the final person to qualify for the top ten but Zach King went on to win the prize.

100% UNOFFICIAL

Jake Paul has a pretty formidable punch, it's not a surprise, then, that Tareq asked for $20,000!

3

Jake Paul

Logan's little brother shocked his YouTube rival with a video called 'I Flew To MrBeast's House & Knocked On His Door.' Jake really did surprise the entire Beast Gang with a North Carolina visit they knew nothing about. They worked together again when Tareq let Jake punch him in the chest ... for $20,000!

Ninja and MrBeast share a love of video game *League of Legends*— and have played against each other!

5

Ninja

MrBeast's favorite game is *League of Legends*. So he and gaming favorite Ninja went head to head at an event called Ultimate Crown! Team Beast came out on top, winning $150,000. But their rivalry is very much a friendly one. When Ninja was doing a charity fundraiser in *Fortnite*, MrBeast stunned him with a donation of $50,000!

4

Mythpat

Mithilesh Patankar is an Indian YouTuber famed for his enthusiastic reaction clips. MrBeast recruited him as an alternative voice on 'I Survived 7 Days In An Abandoned City'! You can hear him by changing the language to Zulu. MrBeast also appears in one of Mythpat's videos, too. He tries Mythpat's first language in 'MrBeast Spoke To Me In Hindi'!

MrBeast and Mythpat have done video (or audio!) collaborations together.

57

Happy Birthday, MrBeast

All you need to know about 7 May—the day MrBeast was born!

Ship Shape

One of the most famous movies ever was number one on the day that MrBeast was born! *Titanic* stars American actor Leonardo DiCaprio and British favorite Kate Winslet. It's set on board the Titanic, which sank after hitting an iceberg in 1912. The film came out in 1997 but was still popular enough to be number one six months later!

Aqua Splash

Norwegian pop group Aqua was number one in the UK music charts on MrBeast's date of birth. The track was 'Turn Back Time,' from the movie *Sliding Doors*. You might not have heard of that one but will definitely recognize their most famous hit: 'Barbie Girl'! The USA number one spot was held by boy band Next, with 'Too Close.'

Birthday Party Guestlist

These are some of the celebs who share MrBeast's birthday!

Icy Wicy (TikTok Star)
Tommy Fury (Boxer)
Kevin Owens (Wrestler)
Faker (eSports Player)
Elijah Nelson (Actor)
Sarah Baska (Influencer)
Jake Bongiovi (Model)
Melody Valadez (Influencer)
Snow Wife (Singer)
TheStradman (Influencer)

Future Stars

Wondering what other famous celebs were doing when MrBeast was born? Taylor Swift was eight years old and living on a Christmas tree farm in Pennsylvania. Dwayne Johnson, meanwhile, was the WWE's Intercontinental Champion and just starting his rise to fame as The Rock. As for the Beast Gang: Kris was one year old and the rest weren't born yet!

Video Blackout

Incredibly, YouTube didn't even exist on the day MrBeast was born. The video platform didn't launch until February 7th, 2005—when he was already six years old!

Hello, Britney

The Internet was slow and expensive in 1998. That didn't stop Britney Spears from being the year's breakthrough star. ' ... Baby One More Time' was a smash hit across the globe. The biggest movies included *Godzilla, Dr. Dolittle,* and *A Bug's Life.* France won the World Cup, stunning favorites Brazil with a 3-0 victory in the final.

Scarlett Debut

As well as MrBeast, some iconic entertainment favorites also arrived on May 7th. *Iron Man 2* was released on this day in 2010. It was Scarlett Johansson's first appearance as Black Widow. Shakira's super catchy song 'Waka Waka (It's Time For Africa)' also arrived on the same day, in the same year!

100% UNOFFICIAL

ALL ABOUT Celebrity Friends

The Beast Gang aren't MrBeast's only famous pals. Over the years, he's also become friendly with this brilliant bunch ...

Pete Davidson

Actor and comedian Pete is well known to American fans, as he's made plenty of appearances on legendary comedy show *Saturday Night Live*. He hung out with MrBeast on the '$1 vs $1,000,000,000 Yacht' video. As well as trying out a $50 million boat, he tasted Feastables. The verdict? "It's better than any other chocolate!"

Pete Davidson got to hang out with the Beast Gang in their yacht video and tried Feastables!

Leonardo DiCaprio's company created a documentary series that showcased people changing the world, and featured clips of MrBeast's charity work!

Leonardo DiCaprio

The *Inception* star initially gave MrBeast a shout out on X. MrBeast later told the Flagrant podcast how they met in person: "There's this super exclusive event where there's all these really rich and famous people ... at dinner, they just pair you up with random people so you meet new people and he was the one at the table!"

Tom Brady

The greatest NFL player ever has appeared in two MrBeast videos and provided an all-time highlight in '$1 vs $1,000,000,000 Yacht.' Tom said he would come out of retirement if he could hit a drone with one throw of a football. Sure enough, the drone was dispatched into the sea first time. He's not un-retired just yet, though!

MrBeast flew a drone over the ocean and Tom Brady threw a football directly at it!

Joey Chestnut

The best competitive eater on the planet is MrBeast's go-to guy for food challenges. Joey has appeared in videos wolfing down burgers and pizza, and made a fascinating appearance in 'I Built Willy Wonka's Chocolate Factory.' He explained how to eat competitively, by drinking water straight after a mouthful.

Joey Chestnut has won MrBeast challenges, food challenges, and a Guinness World Record!

100% UNOFFICIAL

KSI took part in MrBeast's challenges and then played soccer with him in Sidemen FC's team.

SIDEMEN

MrBeast's crew faced off with KSI and pals across a series of $1 million challenges. The Honeycomb Maze was exactly what it sounds like—a maze shaped like honeycomb! And guards in bee costumes chased down players as they rushed to find the correct exit. KSI fought back against a bee, then kicked open the wrong door! In Gridiron, players had to catch a touchdown as fast as possible without getting blocked by the other team. MrBeast and pals came out on top, winning 4-1.

TOP FIVE
Animal Moments

MrBeast has rescued dogs on multiple occasions but likes to set the Beast Gang animal-based challenges, too!

1. I Saved 100 Dogs From Dying

Many of MrBeast's kindest videos feature unwanted pets. MrBeast relocated 100 abandoned dogs to a wonderful dog sanctuary. An enthusiastic team of walkers, trainers, and backscratchers kept the hounds happy as they awaited new owners. MrBeast even gave every dog free pet food and insurance. In a magical moment, three-legged dog Buffett was re-homed and given a custom prosthetic limb.

The Beast Gang made Buffett's new owner very happy!

2. Would You Sit In Snakes For $10,000?

The team competed in some crazy challenges to win money for their moms. Kris sat in a bathtub of snakes and won $10,000. MrBeast's sound guy Jeff then won $9,340 from a box of cockroaches! It wasn't all about animals, though. Regina had to pop a balloon with a nail in sixty seconds, while blindfolded, to win a new car.

Kris bravely sat in a bath full of snakes after Chandler had to walk away from fear!

100% UNOFFICIAL

4 I Adopted Every Dog In A Dog Shelter

Monica, Zeppelin, and Gumpy are all names you'll become familiar with while watching this vid. They're three of the hounds rehomed by MrBeast, thanks to a dedicated marketing campaign. He put up flyers and massive billboards to attract animal lovers to the shelter. Potential owners gradually dropped in and, as they adopted new pets, MrBeast gave them cash, pet food, and toys!

The Beast Gang became very attached to the dogs in the shelter, before helping them find homes.

3 We Helped Paralyzed Dogs Run Again

In this video, MrBeast sent reps Darren and Dan to Thailand to support a dog rescuer called Michael. The country has two million strays and Michael can't help them all. As well as giving money to Michael's shelter, MrBeast built a new wing for 300 additional dogs and donated a state-of-the-art anaesthetic machine and a shiny truck. The generosity made Michael cry.

5 Would You Swim With Sharks For $100,000?

MrBeast chucked a backpack containing $100,000 into the shark-infested sea. Thankfully they were friendly and Kris completed the challenge with ease, and gave the winnings to a fan! The same video got trickier when MrBeast put two cases of cash on the other side of a river infested with alligators! Tareq and Chandler said no but animal expert Brian tip-toed across to grab $20,000!

Michael started an organization named The Man That Rescues Dogs to help the thousands of animals in need.

MrBeast took his friends out to shark-infested waters and threw a backpack overboard!

MrBeast's Best Quotes

Everyone can learn from MrBeast's rise to greatness. These are some of his most inspirational words of wisdom!

Although he's doing his dream job, MrBeast has found that being super famous can have some drawbacks:

"I can't be in crowds, I can't watch a movie unless I buy every ticket [in the cinema], or people are going to film me the whole time. I always have to be on guard—I'm known for carrying around money … you're always on."

MrBeast discussed privacy with YouTubers Colin and Samir.

MrBeast is known as one of the most generous celebrities of our time.

"One of the reasons I like giving away money is I just like to see how people react."

In an interview with Paypal Honey, he explained the joy he gets from real people receiving wads of cash.

MrBeast shared this interesting behind-the-scenes insight about his content creation on X:

"Whether it be ideas, sets, editing, humor, coloring, scale, thumbnails, lighting, hiring, etc you can always improve something."

He's famous for wanting every video to be the best it can be, and he takes that seriously—he's even been known to delete some completed videos without ever posting them!

The videos that MrBeast posts online aren't the only ideas that he creates. To get to those final videos, he has to come up with a lot of weird and wacky ones first!

"What if we got all the top creators together I … [and] we all just uploaded a video of us eating cereal and no context to confuse the world."

MrBeast unveiled this unusual future idea on X.

64

100% UNOFFICIAL

The biggest YouTube star has some ambitious plans for his future.

> "I hopefully will make tens of millions of dollars through YouTube, invest it, turn it into hundreds of millions and then, before I die, do fun things with it."

He said in an interview with Paypal Honey.

When you become famous, people's opinions of you can change. In a YouTube short, MrBeast said:

> "You're crazy until you're successful. Then you're a genius."

MrBeast's recent videos are different from those he made early in his career.

> "People want to see a more natural me … I don't have to scream constantly to hold people's attention."

He told YouTube creators Colin and Samir.

When MrBeast started out, he put literally everything he had into his channels.

> "My mindset was just, reinvest everything I make—every time I got a pay check, that was the month's budget."

He shared this financial approach in an interview with fellow influencer Casey Neistat.

Always aware of the impact he has on his viewers, MrBeast warns new content creators on the risks involved in starting out:

> "It's painful to see people quit their job/drop out of school to make content full time before they're ready. For every person like me that makes it, thousands don't."

This advice was shared on X.

Although his life is crazy at times, he's commented about how it surprises him.

> "I just walked past two random guys casually debating how much money MrBeast makes and they didn't notice me."

He posted on X after going under the radar in public.

65

ALL ABOUT MrBeast's Projects

You know his YouTube videos. You've read about his food and charity work. Over the years, MrBeast has fit all this in, too!

Beast Games

MrBeast's latest mega project is the biggest of his career! It's called *Beast Games* and is being broadcast on Prime Video. 1,000 contestants are lined up to compete for a $5 million cash prize. It's the biggest in the history of both television and streaming! "My goal is to make the greatest show possible and prove YouTubers and creators can succeed on other platforms," says MrBeast.

Finger On The App

This was a special MrBeast challenge. Anyone in the world could play it from home! You had to download the app to your phone, then keep your finger on the screen for as long as possible. Four people shared $20,000 each after lasting over seventy hours!

Finger On The App 2

You can guess what this one involved! The sequel to Finger On The App added an even bigger main prize, of $100,000. 1.2 million people immediately downloaded it, taking it straight to number one! X user Swagbacon123 lasted fifty-one hours and won the money.

100% UNOFFICIAL

Roku TV Channel

American viewers have their own MrBeast TV channel! It's found on a streaming service called Roku. It shows a selection of his classic videos and is free to those who have Roku. Sadly, it hasn't arrived to viewers outside of the USA yet. Fingers crossed it'll go global soon!

US viewers can scroll through the MrBeast channel on Roku and watch some of his biggest videos.

The video game controller has a space for Apple phones to be slotted into.

Backbone One

Did you know MrBeast helped to make a gaming controller? It attaches to Apple phones so that playing games feels more like using a Nintendo Switch than a smart device. It's considered a recommended game pad for Xbox Cloud Gaming! Other YouTubers who backed the project included Preston and Kwebbelkop.

These teeny tiny Beast Gang vinyl figures from Youtooz are now very hard to find!

Vinyl Figures

Toy company Youtooz released official MrBeast vinyl figures in 2023! Three characters were available: MrBeast, Chandler, and Kris. Boxes contained random gold tickets. Fans who found one got a life-size figure! They're now very rare.

TOP FIVE
Food Frenzies

Whether it's chowing down on pricey pizza, or building a real-life chocolate factory, MrBeast loves a food-tastic challenge ...

HUNGRY FOR MORE? MrBeast's love of all things foodie led him to create his own chocolate company! Read more on page 24.

Halfway through the vid, MrBeast, Kris and Chandler changed into suave suits to match the moment.

Gordon Ramsey created a tasty and tempting breakfast sandwich that MrBeast couldn't turn down.

1
I Ate A $70,000 Golden Pizza

Everyone has a favorite pizza topping: pepperoni, ham and pineapple, olives ... But for this vid, MrBeast tried a pizza with an ounce of gold covering the crust! Added to that was parmesan béchamel, Japanese beef, foie gras, white truffles, and caviar. Kris especially loved the cheese, and said "I'm pretty sure my life has peaked". They couldn't finish it, so donated $20,000 to a food bank instead!

2
I Didn't Eat Food For 30 Days

Could you go a month without food? MrBeast tried to in this horrendously hungry challenge! It's important not to try this one at home, obviously. One really tough part of the challenge was promoting Feastables without taking a bite. MrBeast made it to an incredible fourteen days before celebrity chef Gordon Ramsey tempted him to chomp a breakfast sandwich. As punishment, Kris had to shave his head!

100% UNOFFICIAL

3. Going Through The Same Drive Thru 1,000 Times

The team had to order from the same Hardees fast food restaurant 1,000 times in one day. If they failed, they had to work there! Along the way, they scarfed down chips, cookies and apple pie. Kris managed to pay for one order by mowing the lawn! To save on wastage (and eating till they were sick!), they ordered a lot of bottled water and orange juice, so they could be donated later. The team finally got it done, after fourteen hours!

MrBeast dressed for the occasion in Willy Wonka's famous top hat and velvet jacket.

The team took it in turns to drive through the queue—they had 1,000 different trips to make!

4. I Built Willy Wonka's Chocolate Factory

Take a classic kids' book. Add a movie reinvention. Top it off with some MrBeast magic. What do you get? A batch of challenges set in a chocolate factory, just like Roald Dahl imagined! Obviously there was a chocolate river, and Gordon Ramsey popped up again to judge which one of three contestants would win the entire factory! The contestants had forty-five minutes to cook the best dessert. The winning bake was a confetti cake with a banana boat in the middle—and a chocolate waterfall!

5. I Ate The World's Largest Slice Of Pizza

Oh. My. Gosh. For this one, MrBeast took on a 6-foot piece of pizza that was even bigger than Karl! He was joined by Joey Chestnut, the fastest competitive eater on the planet. Joey destroyed his half of the pizza in under thirty-three minutes, and even refused an offer of $10,000 to slow down. MrBeast, Kris and Chandler struggled so much on their half that they asked Karl and Tyler to help—and then tapped in Jackson and Dustin—but they still couldn't finish! Mmmm, hungry now …

The 6-foot pizza slice that defeated MrBeast and six members of the team.

MrBeast's Essential Trivia

Still wanna know even more about MrBeast? Here are twelve more essential facts and stats to memorize!

1
Legendary composer Hans Zimmer composed the soundtrack to 'I Spent 50 Hours in Antarctica.' He's known for amazing movie music like *The Lion King*, *Dune*, and *The Dark Knight*!

2
MrBeast has promised to release a video in 2025 called 'Hi Me In 10 Years.' It was recorded when he was fifteen and features MrBeast predicting how many subscribers he'd have a decade later!

3
When MrBeast met John Cena, he posted a photo with the caption "I couldn't find someone to take a picture with me." It was a hilarious play on Cena's catchphrase: "You can't see me!"

4
As well as English, MrBeast videos can be watched in Arabic, Bangla, French, Hindi, Indonesian, Japanese, Korean, Portuguese, Russian, Spanish, Thai, Turkish, and Vietnamese!

5
MrBeast purchased the island from 'I Bought A Private Island' for $730,000. Its official name is Golding Cay Island but Chandler jokingly renamed it Jeff!

MrBeast was really excited to meet one of his favorite actors, John Cena.

MrBeast hired this Oscar-winning movie composer to work on one of his videos.

100% UNOFFICIAL

3 Going Through The Same Drive Thru 1,000 Times

The team had to order from the same Hardees fast food restaurant 1,000 times in one day. If they failed, they had to work there! Along the way, they scarfed down chips, cookies and apple pie. Kris managed to pay for one order by mowing the lawn! To save on wastage (and eating till they were sick!), they ordered a lot of bottled water and orange juice, so they could be donated later. The team finally got it done, after fourteen hours!

The team took it in turns to drive through the queue—they had 1,000 different trips to make!

MrBeast dressed for the occasion in Willy Wonka's famous top hat and velvet jacket.

4 I Built Willy Wonka's Chocolate Factory

Take a classic kids' book. Add a movie reinvention. Top it off with some MrBeast magic. What do you get? A batch of challenges set in a chocolate factory, just like Roald Dahl imagined! Obviously there was a chocolate river, and Gordon Ramsey popped up again to judge which one of three contestants would win the entire factory! The contestants had forty-five minutes to cook the best dessert. The winning bake was a confetti cake with a banana boat in the middle— and a chocolate waterfall!

5 I Ate The World's Largest Slice Of Pizza

Oh. My. Gosh. For this one, MrBeast took on a 6-foot piece of pizza that was even bigger than Karl! He was joined by Joey Chestnut, the fastest competitive eater on the planet. Joey destroyed his half of the pizza in under thirty-three minutes, and even refused an offer of $10,000 to slow down. MrBeast, Kris and Chandler struggled so much on their half that they asked Karl and Tyler to help—and then tapped in Jackson and Dustin—but they still couldn't finish! Mmmm, hungry now ...

The 6-foot pizza slice that defeated MrBeast and six members of the team.

69

MrBeast's Essential Trivia

Still wanna know even more about MrBeast? Here are twelve more essential facts and stats to memorize!

1
Legendary composer Hans Zimmer composed the soundtrack to 'I Spent 50 Hours in Antarctica.' He's known for amazing movie music like *The Lion King*, *Dune*, and *The Dark Knight*!

2
MrBeast has promised to release a video in 2025 called 'Hi Me In 10 Years.' It was recorded when he was fifteen and features MrBeast predicting how many subscribers he'd have a decade later!

3
When MrBeast met John Cena, he posted a photo with the caption "I couldn't find someone to take a picture with me." It was a hilarious play on Cena's catchphrase: "You can't see me!"

4
As well as English, MrBeast videos can be watched in Arabic, Bangla, French, Hindi, Indonesian, Japanese, Korean, Portuguese, Russian, Spanish, Thai, Turkish, and Vietnamese!

MrBeast was really excited to meet one of his favorite actors, John Cena.

MrBeast hired this Oscar-winning movie composer to work on one of his videos.

5
MrBeast purchased the island from 'I Bought A Private Island' for $730,000. Its official name is Golding Cay Island but Chandler jokingly renamed it Jeff!

100% UNOFFICIAL

6
His mom does more than just guest star in his videos! She's also his official financial advisor. Given that he's worth around $500 million, it's pretty important to have someone he completely trusts in charge!

7
He says the first app he opens on his phone every morning is X!

8
If an Uber driver asks what his job is, he tells them he works at McDonald's!

9
The hardest challenge he's ever done was being buried alive.

This global fast food restaurant is MrBeast's cover when he's asked about his job.

10
He goes through the dictionary and picks out random words as inspiration for video content. "It works actually better than you would think," he told fellow YouTube creator Marques Brownlee.

11
He likes ketchup on his steak—but says restaurants yell at him for asking for it!

How would MrBeast's celebrity chef friend, Gordon Ramsey feel about eating ketchup with steak?

One of MrBeast's favorite video games, *Minecraft*, gives players a huge world to build and explore in.

12
His original inspiration to become a YouTuber was the channel WoodysGamertag, which focused on *Minecraft* and *Call of Duty*.

71

Credits

Front Cover Pictures Alamy: Sipa US / Alamy Stock Photo

Page 6 Pictures: Tinseltown / Shutterstock.com
Page 7 Pictures: Shutterstock: Matthew Nichols1 / Shutterstock.com
Page 11 Pictures: Shutterstock: PhotopankPL / Shutterstock.com, Mossaab Shuraih / Shutterstock.com
Page 12 Words: YouTube, Anthony Padilla; YouTube, MrBeast
Page 16 Pictures: Shutterstock: KSwinicki / Shutterstock.com, Chad Robertson Media / Shutterstock.com
Page 17 Pictures: Alamy: M4OS Photos / Alamy Stock Photo, Shutterstock: Kathy Hutchins / Shutterstock.com, ZikG / Shutterstock.com
Page 20 Pictures: Alamy: Kathy Hutchins / Alamy Stock Photo, Erik Pendzich / Alamy Stock Photo
Page 21 Pictures: Alamy: Kathy Hutchins / Alamy Stock Photo, Image Press Agency/Alamy Live News, Sipa US/ Alamy Live News
Page 23 Pictures: Shutterstock: Joe Seer / Shutterstock.com, Litepix / Shutterstock.com
Page 24 Words: Twitter/X, MrBeast
Pictures: Shutterstock: Billy F Blume Jr / Shutterstock.com
Page 25 Pictures: Alamy: © Frank Gunn/The Canadian Press via Credit: Zuma Press/Alamy Live News, z1b / Alamy Stock Photo
Page 27 Words: YouTube, MrBeast
Page 29 Pictures: Shutterstock: Grindstone Media Group / Shutterstock.com, SPF / Shutterstock.com
Page 28 Words: Twitter/X, MrBeast
Page 30 Words: YouTube, MrBeast
Page 31 Words: YouTube, MrBeast
Page 35 Pictures: Alamy: Jennifer Graylock/Alamy Live News
Page 36 Pictures: Shutterstock: Chad Robertson Media / Shutterstock.com, WS-Studio / Shutterstock.com
Page 37 Pictures: Shutterstock: Fred Duval / Shutterstock.com, Popova Valeriya / Shutterstock.com, Sharkshock / Shutterstock.com
Page 39 Words: YouTube, MrBeast
Page 40 Pictures: Alamy: © Paramount Pictures / Courtesy Everett Collection
Page 41 Words: Kung Fu Panda 4
Pictures: Alamy © DreamWorks Animation/ Entertainment Pictures/ZUMAPRESS.com, FlixPix / Alamy Stock Photo
Page 42 Words: YouTube, MrBeast

Page 47 Words: Twitter/X, MrBeast; YouTube, PayPal Honey
Pictures: Shutterstock: Glebiy / Shutterstock.com, Sean Pavone / Shutterstock.com, Septiwn / Shutterstock.com, maicasaa / Shutterstock.com
Page 48 Words: Reddit, vdnx
Pictures: Shutterstock: Andrew Marek / Shutterstock.com
Page 49 Pictures: Shutterstock: tony cad / Shutterstock.com, Adriana Iacob / Shutterstock.com
Page 52 Pictures: Shutterstock: Fotokon / Shutterstock.com
Page 53 Pictures: Shutterstock: PhotopankPL / Shutterstock.com, nomadFra / Shutterstock.com, Michal Dziedziak / Shutterstock.com
Page 54 Pictures: Getty: Megan Briggs / Stringer, Chris Unger/Zuffa LLC
Page 55 Words: Twitter/X, MrBeast
Pictures: Alamy: Sipa US/Alamy Live News
Page 56 Pictures: Alamy: Billy Bennight/AdMedia/ Newscom/Alamy Live News
Page 57 Pictures: Alamy: Anthony Behar/Sipa USA, Kathy Hutchins / Alamy Stock Photo, Sipa US/Alamy Live News
Page 58 Pictures: Shutterstock: Featureflash Photo Agency / Shutterstock.com, Kraft74 / Shutterstock.com
Page 59 Pictures: Alamy: Fabio Diena / Alamy Stock Photo, Xavier Collin/Image Press Agency, © Paramount Pictures - Marvel Studios
Page 60 Words: YouTube, Flagrant; YouTube, MrBeast
Pictures: Shutterstock: Kathy Hutchins / Shutterstock.com
Page 61 Pictures: Alamy: Michael Tubi/Alamy Live News, Newscom/Alamy Live News
Page 64 Words: YouTube, Colin and Samir; Twitter/X, MrBeast; YouTube, PayPal Honey
Page 65 Words: YouTube, PayPal Honey; YouTube, MrBeast; YouTube, Colin and Samir; Twitter/X, MrBeast; YouTube, Casey Neistat
Page 66 Words: Prime Video
Pictures: Shutterstock: RODWORKS / Shutterstock.com
Page 67 Pictures: Shutterstock: Matthew Nichols1 / Shutterstock.com
Page 68 Words: YouTube, MrBeast
Page 70 Words: Twitter/X, MrBeast
Pictures: Shutterstock: Tinseltown / Shutterstock.com DFree / Shutterstock.com
Page 71 Words: YouTube, Marques Brownlee
Pictures: Shutterstock: FoodAndPhoto / Shutterstock.com, Craig Russell / Shutterstock.com